Level Nine

LIANA BROOKS

OTHER WORKS

Fey Lights
Prime Sensations

HEROES AND VILLAINS

Even Villains Fall In Love
Even Villains Go To The Movies
Even Villains Have Interns
Even Villains Play The Hero (books 1 – 3 omnibus)

TIME AND SHADOWS MYSTERIES

The Day Before
Convergence Point
Decoherence

FLEET OF MALIK

Bodies In Motion
Change of Momentum
For Every Action (forthcoming)

Find other works by the author at
www.lianabrooks.com

Level Nine

INKLET #19

LIANA BROOKS

Inkprint PRESS

www.inkprintpress.com

Print ISBN: 978-1-925825-18-3
eBook ISBN: 9781386225652

www.inkprintpress.com

National Library of Australia Cataloguing-in-Publication Data
Liana Brooks 1982 –
Level Nine
42 p.
ISBN: 978-1-925825-18-3
Inkprint Press, Canberra, Australia
1. Fiction—Short Stories 2. Fiction—Science Fiction—Action & Adventure

First Print Edition: October 2019
Cover design © Inkprint Press
Interior art © Amy Laurens

LEVEL NINE

ANDREA STOOD AT THE EDGE OF THE clearing studying the opposing force. She counted three hundred and seven killerbots loaded with every armament the engineers could think of. They stood there, a lethal wall of AI menace separating her from her goal.

The bushes behind her shook. Puzzled, she watched a man roll into view. Lasers seared the bush, setting it on fire. The man stood up and brushed the dirt away. He looked... wholesome.

Andrea tried to find another word. Crazy? He only had a small destabilizer, no armor, no vanguard of cohorts.

"Hello." He smiled.

Andrea smiled back. "All alone?"

"No one else could play today. You?"

"Flying solo," Andrea confirmed.

"Can't figure out how to get past?" the man asked.

"I can't figure out how to get past without cheating," she corrected. "This is only level seven, I've gone past a dozen times. But I always cheat."

"You can't cheat the game."

"You can," Andrea said. "You aren't supposed to, but you can."

"How?" He looked over the massed infantry of death in confusion.

She knew what he was thinking. The gate leading to level eight was plain to see. All you had to do was charge in, kill all of the killerbots in your way, and run through the level gate.

"If you're very fast..." he began.

"No. Just lazy. Watch." Andrea lifted a small stone; she weighed it in her hand. "Watch." She threw the rock, arcing it into the center of the killerbots.

As a unit, the droids turned and opened fire on each other. Within seconds there was nothing left of the wall of death but the hiss of cooling metal.

"Impossible. It must be a system glitch. They are programmed so they can't attack each other."

"They each attack the rock and most of them miss," Andrea said. "If the rock shatters it gets even better. Then they start shooting at the fragments."

"And they don't reset?" Intrigue and respect were written on the man's face.

"No," Andrea said. "It really is cheating though. I feel guilty just walking past their charred corpses."

"Is a melted droid really a corpse?" he asked.

Andrea punched a code into the controller at her wrist and the level reset.

The bushes shook again. This time an entire band of warriors rushed in, armed to the teeth and yelling.

"You need to go through?" one asked.

Andrea looked at the first stranger; he shook his head. "We just reset the level to try a different tactic. Not enough challenge the first time," she said.

"Mind if we charge through?" one of the heavily-armed men asked.

"Go for it."

Andrea and the wholesome man with the charming smile watched as the band of berserkers rushed the killerbots.

"We could try that," he suggested.

"They lost two people."

"Ah, good point. The odds aren't in our favor."

"Any suggestions?" Andrea asked as the level reset yet again.

The man picked up a rock.

They stepped through the level eight gate casually—almost too casually. Andrea had to grab the man by his shirt to keep him from making a fatal mistake.

"Trip wires under the leaves on the path," she explained.

"Ah," he looked down at the jungle path in front of them. "How do we avoid the trip wires?"

"See the wood planks outlining the path?"

He looked at the narrow span of wood. "Yes."

"Stay on that until we hit the clearing." Andrea balanced easily on the beam and waited for him to follow before she began moving. "The wires trigger the killerbots and skydroids on the other end. If you don't trigger the wires the 'bots don't come out."

"I thought the rules said you had to stay on the path," the man said.

"The rules were written by the same people who designed the killerbots. Think about it."

"Good point. I suppose they aren't rooting for the gamers."

"If they are, I've never noticed."

They moved through the artificial jungle, listening to the sounds ahead. A battle raged and fell suddenly silent.

"Do you think the berserkers died?"

"Charging doesn't work on this level. I've seen lots of groups try that and it never works. Level seven is the last one you can survive by charging. By eight, you need actual tactics."

"Do you play a lot?" the man asked politely.

Andrea looked at him, weighing her possible responses. "I play when I can, but it isn't often."

"Do you always come alone?"

"Do you?"

The man laughed. "I'm not trying to pry. I'm harmless. Really. And yes, I usually play alone."

"But you pick up the odd damsel in distress if you happen upon them?"

"Nope. Never met one. Although I don't mind picking up beautiful women who know how to cheat two levels in a row."

"Do you meet many?" Andrea asked.

"Nope. But after I met you, who else could I need?" His smile was dazzling.

Andrea snorted. "Nice line. But what you're going to want is someone who knows how to get past level nine, because I don't."

They stepped into an empty clearing with monumental buildings on each side. The doors to the buildings were closed, locking in the hordes of death.

The level gate loomed ahead of them.

"Suggestions?" the man asked.

"Level nine is dark, pitch black. Outside light sources don't work. The level gate is to the left but there's a cliff and a river between you and the gate. I've died in each of them. And there's a couple of killerbots. It never seems like a huge number but there are enough."

"Maybe we should try splitting up? One go left, the other go right?" he suggested.

"Bad plan. There are synergy bombs. If you and your buddy stand on the corresponding demolition plants at the same time, everyone in the level dies."

"Great." He checked his charge. "So, want to try again if we die?"

Andrea blinked at the thought. "I've got to get to work."

"Maybe we can meet up later? Where are you at?"

"Tetraterren, Alpha Side," Andrea said. "You?"

"Homely." A planet on the far side of the system.

"Thank goodness for faster than light relays, right?"

"Right."

"Our best bet is to try not to die," Andrea said. "Failing that, remember every detail you can so you can map the level when you die."

"When are you coming to play next?" the man asked.

Andrea shrugged. "I don't know." She stepped into the darkness of level nine.

Five minutes later, simulated leg broken, a killerbot honed in on Andrea. She shot out its sensors, trying to buy herself a few more seconds in the game.

Light flashed, a fire flare. "I'll find you!" the stranger shouted as he died.

The killerbots fired. Andrea died. The black and green grid of the ten-by-ten game room replaced the encircling dark of level nine. Andrea checked her watch. "Flippers!" Her shuttle for the space station took off in ten minutes.

She raced out the door, stripping her game suit as she went. She tossed the controls to the tech outside with a smile and grabbed her raincoat from the hangar.

"Good game?" the tech asked as she pushed herself out the door.

"The best!"

He'd find her—or she'd find him. And together, they'd figure out a way to conquer level nine.

THE MAKING OF
LEVEL NINE

Do you ever have reoccurring dreams? I do. And some of them are very odd.

Level Nine was one of those dreams that hit in college. Every few weeks I'd have the same dream where I was in a game simulation with friends from high school. There were killer robots and a trip wire and I kept dying!

The dream finally stopped when I solved the level.

One of these days I might make a book out of the idea, but for now it's a short story that's perfect for bedtime.

Read more by Liana Brooks!

FLEET OF MALIK
BODIES IN MOTION
CHAPTER ONE

THE PROBLEM WITH VACATIONS, Selena reflected as she adjusted her sweater outside Cargo Blue, was that reality was always waiting at the end. A quick search of the local security cameras found one that showed the peeling sunburn on her right shoulder blade.

Such was the curse of pale-skinned, ship-born Fleet personnel. Anytime she left the foggy belts covering the city of Tarrin, she barbecued like a shrimp, no matter how much sunscreen she applied. Otherwise, she'd flee even further from the Fleet Enclave and make her home on the equatorial beaches of the planet they were trapped on.

She panned the camera and checked her left shoulder. Black ink made a star-scape that disguised three silver scars as shooting stars. The painting covered her shoulder blade and part of her upper arm. As the artist had promised, the skin-paint had kept her from burning as much, though it still had the over-stretched feel of a burn. With a few adjustments, her uniform covered most of the temporary art; it would keep her from having to explain to her colleagues.

Her forearm warmed, a warning that someone was about to contact her through the tech implant tucked between her radius and ulna.

She hesitated too long and the call came through, a persistent ping against her skull as the phantom image of her best friend floated on the edge of her vision.

Selena turned off the visual receiver and answered. "Genevieve," she said with a smile as the image of her vivacious, red-headed friend appeared floating against the backdrop of landing gear that supported the grounded fleet.

A grounder would have thought she was talking to herself, but grounders wouldn't set foot near the neo-city-state of

Enclave. The rocky beach served as a city and tomb for the survivors of the last war.

"Selena!" Gen gushed. "Starcom to Selena. Where are you? I'm covering for now."

"Delayed, but almost there." Selena hoped Gen wouldn't hear the lie. She'd been standing in the shadows of the Enclave pub for nearly a quarter hour.

"The *Lorenza* could get here faster," Gen said, referencing a long-dead ship whose crew were found skeletonized at their stations. Gen blew hair off her face. "Stars above, you're an hour late. The whole fleet is flying faster than you."

Selena turned on her visual long enough to roll her eyes at her friend. "Ha, ha, funny. That joke needs to be forcibly retired." Sooner rather than later. The fleet couldn't fly without fuel, and the Malik system they were stranded in held precious few deposits of the orun crystals needed to power the ships.

"If you don't come," Gen said threateningly, "I will teleport to your apartment and drag you out in your pajamas."

"I'm not at home," Selena admitted. And she wouldn't have let her best friend come to her new house if she was.

Gen was smart enough to realize that the small palace Selena had bought in downtown Tarrin wasn't paid for by her official OIA salary. The paygrades for the Office of Imperial Affairs had last been updated when the Malik system was still in contact with the empire, making them 900 years out of date.

Technically, taking a second job wasn't treason, but there were enough people in the fleet who'd see it as a betrayal that keeping it secret felt right. Especially since Gen's captain was one who would scream the loudest.

Gen clapped. "Selena! Stop stalling yer engines and get in here. This isn't some Fleet Tribunal, just our friends. You, me, Carver. I left a message for Marshall. You know. People we like."

The light of understanding dawned. "Carver? This is so you can snuggle up to Perrin Carver without your parents watching?"

"Yes," Gen admitted, not looking the least bit contrite.

"You're only dragging me along so I can cover for you while you make out in a corner, aren't you?" She masked the relief with mock anger. At least Gen wasn't trying to set Selena up with one of her cousins. Or, ancestors forbid, Gen's handsy older brother.

Again.

Gen opened her eyes wide with an innocent smile. "Maybe."

"Gen!" Selena rolled her eyes. "Doesn't he have his own place?"

"Just the bachelor's dorm. The Carvers didn't have any ships except the shuttle his parents crashed in. Making out next door to Mom and Dad? No. And the BOQ? It's so tacky. You can hear everything through those walls."

Selena hid a smile. "I'll be there soon enough."

If Gen ever caught wind of how panicky the thought of a relationship made her, Gen would make it her life's goal to see Selena paired off. And there wasn't a man alive who she could imagine getting close to now.

Her implant helpfully pulled up an image of a tall, broad-shouldered, lean-muscled fighter with skin black as the night between stars and emerald-green eyes.

She pushed the memory away.

Lieutenant Commander Titan Sciarra was striking, intelligent, and had a body she'd cross battle lines for, but he was also out of reach. There was no point in chasing a man who wouldn't give her the time of day.

Another crew shuffled past her into the bar, black patches with silver fists on their shoulders.

It was getting harder to pretend she belonged in Enclave, with the fleet. Once upon a time, she'd known every crew's patch without thinking. She could name captains, their ships and their seconds by rote.

Now she would need to tap into the fleet's information nexus if she wanted to know who they were.

She stopped at the edge of the door to tug her lightest shields into place. A few minor adjustments would keep bugs away, keep beer off her clothes, and prevent anyone from hacking into her implant. They could still send messages, because disallowing that would have raised eyebrows. And they could still hit her. But she could always hit back.

Selena rolled her shoulders and strutted into Cargo Blue. It was a battlefield, but she was the last captain of the Caryll family, and she wasn't going down without a fight.

Whatever crew owned Cargo Blue probably hadn't had much of a decorating budget, but at least they'd stuck with a theme: oversized cargo boxes were piled up to make walls, seating, and tables. Olive-green safety webbing draped from the ceiling between blue lights. Fog used for fire drills on the ships pumped across the floor to hide the concrete beneath.

There was no bouncer at the door, but people were still hanging around the entrance.

As a rule, the fleet was cautious, and the young faces she saw belonged to fleet members who had never ventured outside their own crew more than a few times, even though the fleet had been grounded for nearly three years.

Tables to the left, bar ahead, dance floor to the right... and that meant the back half of the cargo hanger had been partitioned and karaoke would be in the back right corner. After a few minutes of weaving through the human crush, she found Gen, already sitting in Perrin Carver's lap and giggling.

"Selena!" Gen jumped up and hugged her. "I was beginning to worry!"

"How many people are in here?" Selena shouted over the music.

"Everyone under forty?" Gen laughed. With a small hand wave Gen put up a minor sound shield, muting the music. "People are going to stir crazy. Combine that with the anniversary—"

The anniversary.

Today.

The day the war had begun, the day the

united fleet had died.

They'd been dying for four hundred years, well aware that the reserve of orun crystals was depleted and there was no way to move forward with the ships they had.

Old Captain Baular had seen the deposit of orun on the fifth planet as their saving grace. He'd get it even if it meant killing the grounders.

And, coward that he was, he'd ordered his grandson to lead the first attack instead of leading it himself.

That opening skirmish began and ended in the dark, with Titan Sciarra in the infirmary, and five Academy fighters mis-sing or damaged. But by lunch of the next day, every officer belonging to crews allied with the Baulars withdrew.

Seven months later, heated words turned to live rounds.

"Selena?" Gen asked quietly, placing a hand on her arm. "You didn't know the date, did you?"

"I was trying not to think about." If she had, she'd have cut her vacation to the islands early. Maybe even made her pilgrimage to the small cay where she'd ditched her stolen fighter after driving off the attack.

She rolled her shoulder, stretching the deep scars. "It snuck up on me."

"First round, we drink to the Lost Fleet, and all who've gone on to crew it. I'm buying," Gen said with a touch of forced joviality. "Carver's been making friends. Tell her, babe." She pushed Carver's shoulder.

Perrin Carver was tall, broad-shouldered man with shy, hazel eyes that hid a wicked sense of humor.

Selena's heart fluttered just a little at the memory of a time when she'd fancied herself in love with him. He'd been the ideal starsider: intelligent, good-looking, and charismatic. They'd been friends of a sort, but even that relationship had soured when she'd realized he'd been getting close to her so he could learn more about Genevieve Silar.

Carver nodded and held out his hand. "Hi, Selena. How are you?"

She tapped the back of his hand with hers, letting him test her shields. "Good. How's the Starguard?"

"Booming." The commander of the Starguard smiled, white teeth flashing, but there was a tightness around his eyes. "Everyone hears about guardians being allowed outside the Enclave, or working with the Jhandarmi, and I'm drowning in recruiting requests. Captains of larger crews invite me to Captain's Mess so they can introduce me to their best and brightest. Half the time I can't tell if they want me to marry into the crew or take the fleetlings into the guard." His shield was still attached to hers, scanning her as he talked.

All he would get from her was polite interest. Her heartrate didn't spike or dip at the mention of the Jhandarmi. Her smile never flickered.

"Maybe you should lock down Gen," Selena said. "If you had a spouse, no one would try to get you to marry into the crew."

Carver and Gen shared a look, and Gen

sent a ping of information that Selena's implant translated as an ongoing debate over crew name and a place to live.

Carver sent something similar; a picture of his bachelor's quarters and his one ship.

There was no room for them to marry and have a family.

"Enclave is a temporary solution," Selena said out loud. She'd lost the taste for communicating by implant years ago. "If we—"

A heavy hand wrapped around her waist as someone wearing too much cologne stepped far too close to her. "Hello, Selena."

Hollis Silar, one of Gen's many siblings, kissed her temple.

Simultaneously, Selena sighed, sent a shock through her shield to Hollis's hand, and elbowed him in the gut. "Hi, Hollis. I see you're still bathing in cologne rather than water."

He stepped away from her, an easy smile still in place.

It wasn't that Hollis was bad looking;

plenty of women found him handsome.

It was that he was equally affectionate with every woman he saw and he couldn't keep a secret to save his life. Or anyone else's.

He'd chase anyone with a pretty smile and fell in and out of love a couple of times a day.

"Nice to see you too, Selena. Now, everyone, you're all going to look at me, smile, and laugh like I'm my normal, dashing self," he said, his smile never changing. "You haven't been paying attention, but I'm not a member of the Starguard for nothing. We're being watched. Now take your nice drinks from the waitress and keep your eyes on me."

Hollis nodded to the waitress and handed out four cups with bright purple liquid. "Bruised Stars all around. Guaranteed to make you giggle, or so the guy at the bar told me. Although he's a Seutaai, so take it with a shield in place." He handed Selena her drink with a smile, but turned immediately to glance over his shoulder.

"Big brother, who are we looking for?" Gen asked with a slow drawl. "Is it a friend who you might have forgotten to call back after a night out?"

Hollis shook his head. "No, I thought I saw some of the Lee crew. Make that, I'm certain of it."

Selena grimaced. "As long as Rowena isn't here."

"Did you call me?"

Startled, Selena looked up to the face of her least favorite woman: Rowena Lee.

"Hello," Selena said politely. "I see you're still alive. That's..."

Unfortunate.

She nodded and took a slug of her Bruised Star.

Rowena held up a tray of electric blue shots. "My crew thinks I can't out-drink anyone in this bar. I probably can't go toe-to-toe with alcoholics like the Silars here. But No-Shot Selena?" Rowena set the drinks on the table. "I can out-shoot you in the stars or on the ground."

Gen sucked in air between her teeth and sent Selena several urgent pings telling her to ignore the Lees.

Selena muted Gen. "I took plenty of shots in the war. As I recall, I disabled three of your big birds. *Bassi, Aryton, Theoano*... Bang, bang, bang." Selena mimed firing with her finger. "Three shots. Three silent ships."

"Not kills," Rowena said. "A whole war and you never blooded yourself."

That was it, the memory she didn't want to face; the time she'd almost taken Death's claim and risked killing someone outside of war.

"That's uncalled for," Hollis said, trying to step between them. "Selena, why don't we—"

Selena pushed Hollis aside and grabbed the first shot.

She tossed back the potent drink and shattered the glass on the table. "Go suck vacuum, Rowena. You're a pissant yeoman with no hope of command."

"I went to the Academy, same as you, Selena. I fought for the fleet." Rowena slammed a shot back. "You fought for the mud-lickers."

Selena took another shot as the first started to fuzz her judgement. "I prevented the Baulars from committing mass genocide and destroying the civilians along with the fleet."

Rowena took her second shot. A crowd was gathering and that seemed to feed her cruelty. "The Lees survived the war. We're still here. How many Caryll captains are there? Oh, right, one. Can you count that high, No-Shot? You have any idea how easy it would be for me to end you right now?"

Selena took the last two glasses and slammed them both back.

Gen pinged her, giving locations, counts, and identities of the Lee allies in the crowd.

Hollis stepped to her flank, ready to defend her.

She stood, anger burning through her veins. "Sure, your crew outnumbers mine. I guess on paper, it's not really a fair fight, is it, Rowena? But you were trained as a flight leader, and what do Carylls do? Hand-to-hand combat. Maybe I should thin your ranks, starting with one mouthy yeoman.”

Keep reading! Head to:
http://www.inkprintpress.com/
liana-brooks/fleet-of-malik/bodies-
in-motion/

ABOUT THE AUTHOR

LIANA BROOKS loves video games, imaginary worlds, tactical problems, and hanging out with her friends.

When she isn't playing with killer robots, she's at home with her family somewhere in North America and probably too close to a bear for your peace of mind.

She has written the popular *Time and Shadows Mysteries* series about clones and the dangers of time travel; the *Fleet of Malik* series of connected sci-fi romances about re-building after a decades long war; and the cult-following *Heroes and Villains* series of superhero romances.

You can find out more about Liana at her website, www.lianabrooks.com.

INKLETS

Collect them all! Released on the 1st and 15th of each month.

INKLET #001
SEVENTY
LIANA BROOKS

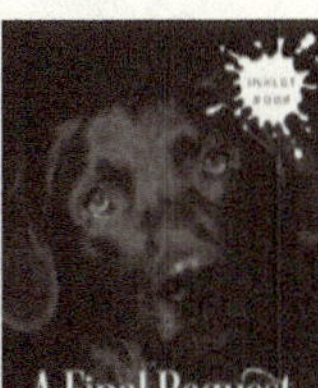

INKLET #008
A Final Request for Mercy
AMY LAURENS

INKLET #009
the kitten psychologist
vs.
the kitten's owners
THEA VAN DIEPEN

Answer the Question
AMY LAURENS

Happily, Red
AMY LAURENS

INKLET #012
the kitten psychologist
tries to be patient
through email
THEA VAN DIEPEN

INKLET #013
DRAGON Tuesday
AMY LAURENS

INKLET #014
RED PLANET REFUGEES
LIANA BROOKS

INKLET #015
the kitten psychologist &
What The Kitten Did
THEA VAN DIEPEN

Cherry Blossom
AMY LAURENS

Alone
AMY LAURENS

the kitten psychologist
& The Kitten
Come To A Conclusion
THEA VAN DIEPEN

LEVEL NINE
LIANA BROOKS

To Dust
AMY LAURENS

Interchange
AMY LAURENS

Emalia's Lanterns
LIANA BROOKS

Dear Santa
AMY LAURENS

The Quilt-Maker's Scrap
AMY L. LAURENS